Most animals, dogs included, cannot bear the direct stare of a human being for long and will look away. But Titus stared back into the Royal eyes, flattening his ears with pleasure and wrinkling his lips in a sort of grin. She seems nice, this Queen person, he thought, and at that instant her Majesty spoke to him once again.

"Titus my boy," said the Queen, "I have a funny feeling that you are going to be a very special dog."

D1352098

Titles available by award-winning author
DICK KING-SMITH

Published by Corgi Pups

Happy Mouseday

Published by Doubleday/Young Corgi

The Adventurous Snail
All Because of Jackson
Billy the Bird
The Catlady
Connie and Rollo
E.S.P.
Funny Frank
The Guard Dog
Horse Pie
Omnibombulator
Titus Rules OK!

Published by Doubleday/Corgi Yearling

A Mouse Called Wolf
Harriet's Hare
Mr Ape

Published by Corgi

The Crowstarver
Godhanger

DICK KING-SMITH

Titus

RULES OK

Illustrated by John Eastwood

TITUS RULES OK
A YOUNG CORGI BOOK : 0 552 55396 4

First published in Great Britain by Doubleday
an imprint of Random House Children's Books

Doubleday edition published 2002
Young Corgi edition published 2003

Set in 16/20pt Bembo Schoolbook

Young Corgi Books are published by Random House Children's Books,
61–63 Uxbridge Road, London W5 5SA,
a division of The Random House Group Ltd,
in Australia by Random House Australia (Pty) Ltd,
20 Alfred Street, Milsons Point, Sydney, NSW 2061, Australia,
in New Zealand by Random House New Zealand Ltd,
18 Poland Road, Glenfield, Auckland 10, New Zealand
and in South Africa by Random House (Pty) Ltd,
Isle of Houghton, Corner of Boundary Road & Carse O'Gowrie,
Houghton 2198, South Africa.

THE RANDOM HOUSE GROUP Limited Reg. No. 954009

www.kidsatrandomhouse.co.uk

A CIP catalogue record for this book is available from the British Library.

Printed and bound in Great Britain by
Cox & Wyman Ltd, Reading, Berkshire.

Chapter One

In an armchair in the great high-ceilinged drawing-room sat a woman, surrounded by dogs. Some sat in other chairs, some on the hearthrug, one, the youngest and not much more than a pup, on the woman's lap.

All the dogs were of the same breed. All of them looked up as the door of the room was opened by a tallish man with a strong nose and receding hair and rather bristly eyebrows, who strode in with a military gait that suggested he might once have been a soldier, or perhaps a sailor.

At sight of him, the youngest dog jumped off the woman's lap and rushed forward, getting between the man's legs and almost tripping him up.

The bristly eyebrows came together in a frown. "Good heavens, Madge!" said the man angrily. "Do we have to have these fat little brutes under our feet all the time?"

The woman rose to her full height (which was not very great). Unlike her husband, she was plump and had thick grey hair set in neat permanent waves.

Like him, she looked angry. "There would be no problem if you looked where you were going," she said in a high voice, "and I'll thank you not to refer to my dogs as fat little brutes. They are not fat. They simply have short legs, like all corgis."

Husband and wife stood glowering at one another in that grumpy way that long-married people sometimes do, but before anything else could be said, there was a knock on the door and into the drawing-room came a footman carrying a tray. This he placed upon a table before withdrawing, backwards.

Once the door was closed, the tallish man said, "You feed 'em too much, Madge, that's the trouble."

"That is your opinion, Philip," said the Queen icily, "which I should be glad if you would keep to yourself. Do you want a cup of coffee?"

"No, thanks, I fancy something stronger," the man said, and he withdrew, frontwards.

The Queen poured herself a cup of coffee, and then, taking from the tray a plate of biscuits, proceeded to feed them to the corgis. "Custard creams, my dears," she said, smiling. "Your favourites." And she gave an extra one to the youngest corgi.

"Not your fault," she said to him. "He wasn't looking where he was going."

Later, when the Queen had finished her coffee and left the room, the mother of the youngest corgi jumped into her chair, warm from the imprint of the Royal bottom, and her son scrambled up beside her.

His name was Titus, and like all young creatures, he was curious about everything. It was the first time he had been allowed into the drawing-room of the Castle, and also the first time he had met the Queen's husband.

"Mum," he said. "Who was that man?"

"The Queen's husband," his mother replied.

" 'Philip', she called him," said Titus.

"Yes. He's Prince Philip, the Duke of Edinburgh."

"Oh," said Titus. "They didn't seem to like each other much."

"I think they do," said his mother. "Their barks are worse than their bites."

"Oh," said Titus. "Mum, you told me she's called Queen Elizabeth the Second."

"Yes."

"What happened to the First?"

"Died. A long time ago."

"Oh," said Titus. "But Mum, if her name's Elizabeth, why does Prince Philip call her Madge?"

"It's his nickname for her," his mother said. "Short for Majesty."

Chapter Two

The door of the great drawing-room now opened once again, and in came the footman to collect the tray on which stood the two cups and saucers, the coffee-pot, and the plate that had held the biscuits.

The footman inspected the tray. One cup had been used, he saw, one not, and, picking up the coffee-pot, he found that it was still half full. He grinned.

"Ta very much, ma'am," he said. "Plenty left for me. But surely you've never scoffed all those custard creams? I could have done with a couple."

Then he looked round the room and saw
ten pairs of bright eyes watching him from
various chairs or from the rug before the
blazing fire. Ten pink tongues licked ten pairs
of lips and ten stumps of tails wagged
hopefully.

"Of course!" said the footman. "I should have known. It wasn't her that ate 'em, it was you greedy little fatties. Treats you better than she treats old Phil, or Charlie, or the rest of 'em, she does. Pity you don't live out in the Far East. They eat dogs out there. You lot would make a proper banquet." And he picked up the tray.

When he had left the room, "Mum," said Titus. "Who was that man?"

"Just a footman," his mother replied.

"Footman?" said Titus. "What was wrong with his feet?"

"Nothing, dear," said his mother. "A footman is one of the servants in the Castle, there are lots of them."

"What's a servant?"

"Someone who looks after you, does whatever he or she is told, fetches and carries, just like that footman brought the tray for the Queen and the Duke."

"But Mum," said Titus. "Why couldn't they fetch their own coffee and biscuits?"

"Oh goodness me, no, Titus!" said his mother. "That would never do. The Queen and Prince Philip have to be looked after. They're not expected to work. When you get a little older, you'll realize that Queen

Elizabeth is the
most important
person in the land.
No-one is more
important than she
is, at least no other
human being."

Titus cocked his ears. "If I'm reading you
right, Mum," he said, "you're saying that
there's an animal that's more important
than the Queen?"

"Several animals," said his mother.
"What sort?"
"Pembrokeshire corgis."
"Us, d'you mean?"

"Yes, Titus," replied his mother. "The Queen, you see, may be responsible for the welfare not just of her family but of all the citizens of the United Kingdom and her realms overseas. But, in her eyes, it is our welfare that is at the top of her priorities and most important to her. She is our servant."

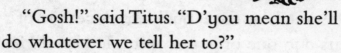

"Gosh!" said Titus. "D'you mean she'll do whatever we tell her to?"

"Certainly," said his mother.

"If I told her to do something, she'd do it, would she, Mum?"

"If you told her in the right way."

"How d'you mean?"

"Politely. Her Majesty does not like being barked at or yapped at. You'll have noticed that just now, when she dished out the biscuits, we all kept as quiet as mice.

Any time you want a biscuit, just go and sit quite silently in front of the Queen and gaze up into her eyes with a pleading look.

And don't ever be tempted to lift a paw and scratch at the Royal legs. A couple of years ago one of your cousins laddered Her Majesty's stockings. Never seen him since."

"Where did he go?"

"He was sent to the Tower of London."

"To be killed?"

"No, no, he was given to one of the warders. But the family felt the disgrace keenly."

"The Royal Family?" asked Titus.

"No, no, our family," said his mother.

"And one other thing, Titus, while I think of it. If ever you're taken short . . ."

"Taken short?"

". . . yes, you know, if you need to, um, cock your leg, or, er, do your business, there is a proper way of going about it if the Queen is in the room. If it's anyone else, it doesn't matter, you can yap your head off or scratch at the door. But if it's the Queen, this is the correct form. You walk to the door – no running, mind, just walk – and sit in front of it and give a little whine – no barking, mind – and you look back at Her Majesty, and then she'll hurry to let you out.

One thing she does *not* like and that's any sort of accident, on the carpets, say, or against the leg of a chair. Our servant she may be, but it's important to treat servants right if you want them to look after you well."

Perhaps because his mother had just been talking about it, Titus suddenly felt that he did indeed need to do something very badly. How awful, he thought, if on this, his first time in the great drawing-room at Windsor Castle, he should offend their servant the Queen by doing it, not on a chair-leg for he had not yet learned to cock his own leg, but on the carpet. Her Majesty would never forgive him!

"Mum!" he cried. "I need a wee!"

Titus's mother, whose registered name was Lady Priscilla of Windsor but who was always called Prissy by Her Majesty, immediately began to bark loudly.

"Mayday! Mayday!" she cried to the other corgis in the room.

"What's up, Prissy?" they all asked.

"It's not what's up," replied Prissy. "It's what will be down unless we hurry. Titus needs to go outside, sharpish. Sound the alarm!" And at this all the other eight dogs began to bark at the tops of their voices.

Quickly the door of the drawing-room was opened and in came a footman. Titus could see that it was not the same one that had come in before to fetch the tray, for that one had had fair curly hair: whereas this one had straight black hair and, as well, a strip of black hair between his nose and his mouth.

By now, Titus was whining in his distress, and the footman, instantly sizing up the situation, picked him up, hurried away down a corridor, opened a side door, and popped the puppy down on the beautifully mown green grass of a lawn outside.

Thankfully Titus squatted down and did an enormous puddle.

Chapter Three

"*What* a good boy!" said a voice from somewhere high above, and man and dog looked up to see the Queen leaning out of an upstairs window.

The black-moustached footman snapped to attention at sight of Her Majesty, while Titus wagged his rump on seeing the woman who, Mum had told him, was their servant.

"Leave the puppy there, John," called the Queen. "I'm coming right down," and in a few moments she came out of the door on to the lawn, and bent down to stroke Titus and pat him and to rub the roots of his ears, something that he found very pleasant.

"Lucky for you that you didn't do all that on my carpets," said the Queen. "You would have been a most unpopular pup." Then she picked Titus up and held him before her face and looked into his eyes.

Most animals, dogs included, cannot bear the direct stare of a human being for long and will look away. But Titus stared back into the Royal eyes, flattening his ears with pleasure and wrinkling his lips in a sort of grin. She seems nice, this Queen person, he thought, and at that instant Her Majesty spoke to him once again.

"Titus my boy," said the Queen, "I have a funny feeling that you are going to be a very special dog."

At that moment there came another voice, a deep voice, from the upstairs window, and Titus looked up to see the Duke of Edinburgh leaning out.

"Telephone, Madge!" he called.

"Well, answer it, Philip, can't you?"

"I have done. It's for you."

"I'm busy," replied the Queen, continuing to stroke Titus. "Who is it, anyway?"

"It's the Prime Minister."

"Bother!" said the Queen. "One wishes sometimes," she said to Titus as she carried him upstairs, "that one was not continually pestered by politicians ringing one up in one's own home. I daresay you'd be surprised to know for instance that what is called the Queen's Speech is not mine at all. The whole thing's written by *my* government, which actually isn't mine anyway. I tell you, Titus, being Queen is a dog's life."

Back in the great drawing-room, Prissy was getting worried. "Titus has been gone an awful long time," she said to the others. "I hope he's not got into any trouble."

In reply, the bitches amongst the corgis said helpful things like "Of course not, dear, he'll be back in a minute, you'll see," and the dogs made unhelpful remarks such as "Ah well, boys will be boys," and "Let's hope the Prince of Wales doesn't come visiting with those terriers of his, they won't half knock the lad about."

So it was with great relief that at last Prissy saw the door open and the Queen enter, carrying Titus, and she ran forward whining anxiously. The Queen put the puppy down on the carpet, and his mother licked his ear.

"Where have you been all this time?" she asked him. "Mummy's been worrying."

"I've been with our servant," Titus said.

"Our servant? Oh, oh you mean Her Majesty?"

"Yes."

"I'm sorry, Prissy," the Queen said. "I would have brought him back sooner, but I had to answer a phone call, and a very long phone call it was, too. Politicians are all the same, they love the sound of their own voices." She rang a bell and another footman appeared, this time a red-headed one.

"Biscuits, please, Patrick," she said.

"Yes, Your Majesty," said the footman. "What kind, ma'am?"

"Custard creams. Oh and two chocolate digestives."

The Queen sat down in her armchair, and when the biscuits came she fed the custard creams to Prissy and the other eight adult dogs, but offered nothing to Titus.

What about me? he thought, and he moved towards the Royal legs. Mustn't scratch at 'em, he thought to himself, I might ladder the Royal stockings.

But I would like to know
if there are any biscuits
left on that plate, and
in an effort to see, he
sat bolt upright on his
fat little bottom, his
front paws held out
imploringly before him.

"That," said the Queen, "is an extremely
clever thing to do. Never before have I had
a corgi that could manage that trick, they
always fall over backwards. Now something
that my great-great-grandmother Queen
Victoria was fond of saying was 'We are
not amused'. But I must tell
you, Titus, that we *are*
amused." And she broke
the two chocolate diges-
tives into pieces and
carefully fed them to the
young corgi who, had either of
them known it, was destined to become the
most famous dog in the land.

Chapter Four

Ever since she was a small girl — then of course known as Princess Elizabeth — the Queen had always been surrounded by corgis. The Royal Family had many other dogs of many other sorts at Buckingham Palace, at Windsor Castle, at Sandringham, at Balmoral in Scotland. But corgis had always been the favourite breed.

Not that the Queen had a particular favourite amongst them, for she treated them all equally, though she might have admitted to a rather special liking for Lady Priscilla of Windsor, the senior member of the present pack. Prissy had had many puppies in her life, but the birth of her last litter had been a time of high drama. Perhaps because of her rather advanced age, the whelping was a difficult one, and an operation was needed to try to save the unborn pups. Three did not survive. One, Titus, did.

From the moment of his birth the Queen took an interest in this, the only surviving child of this last litter of her dear Prissy, which explains why he had been allowed into the great drawing-room of the Castle at a much earlier age than puppies usually were.

Who knows what might have happened
had Titus, so young and untrained, puddled
on the carpet. But he hadn't. Instead he had
asked to go out, and he had done it on the
lawn, and the Queen had seen him do it.
Later, what's more, he had sat bolt upright
on his bottom before her, something no corgi
of hers had ever done before.

"This last puppy of yours is quite a
character," said the Queen to Prissy. "Not
that I believe in favouritism, of course." But
it was not long before a great many
people in the Castle, from the three
footmen, fair-haired, black-
moustached, red-headed, to such
an august person as the
Comptroller of Her Majesty's
Household, noticed that,
wherever the Queen went,
she was now always
accompanied by one
particular young
corgi.

Sometimes he followed at her heels, sometimes she followed at his, but it was soon plain to everyone that, though the Queen was on record as saying that she didn't believe in having favourites, she now had one.

Even her husband noticed. Prince Philip, though fond of dogs in general, did not particularly like corgis. "Always tripping me up," he would say. Now, looking carefully at Titus at teatime one day, he asked, "I say, Madge, isn't that the little brute that nearly had me over a while ago?"

"Yes," said the Queen, "and he's not a brute and you should look where you're going."

"Charles's blasted little terriers are bad enough," said the Duke, "but at least they're nippy enough to get out of the way. Whereas corgis are just designed for tripping people up, bumbling about like they do, fat little beasts. Any more tea in that pot, Madge?"

When the Queen had poured her husband's tea, she took a sugar lump from the bowl and held it out before Titus, who sat straight up on his bottom, eyes fixed upon the treat.

"Never seen one of 'em do that before," said Prince Philip.

"Clever, aren't you, Titus?" said the Queen, and she gave him the sugar lump.

" 'Titus', is he?" said the Duke. "Where are the rest of 'em then, Madge?"

"Oh they're somewhere around," replied the Queen.

"This one's a bit special then, is he?"

"You know I don't have favourites, Philip," said the Queen. "It's just that Titus is an only child, and Prissy's last one at that because I shan't breed from her again, not at her age."

The Duke of Edinburgh drained his cup and stood up. "Be nice if you didn't breed from any of 'em any more, Madge," he said. "That way they'd all die out and I could walk around without falling over 'em. Just hang on to that Titus till I'm out of the room."

Left alone, the Queen rang for a footman to take away the tea things, and when he had done so (it was the black-moustached one), she picked up Titus and sat him on her lap.

"My husband," she said to him, "is not the easiest person in the world to get on with. I mean, I'm fond of him, as I am of my daughter and my three sons, but I'm probably happiest when I'm alone with my dogs."

She looked into Titus's eyes and, once again, he stared back into hers with that confident gaze of his.

"In fact," said the Queen, "I'm possibly happiest when I'm alone with you."

Chapter Five

Hardly were the words out of the Royal
mouth than there came a knock on the
door. It was not the discreet knock that the
footmen usually gave but a loud *rat-a-tat-tat*.

"Bother!" said the Queen to Titus. "Who
can that be?" and she called, "Come in!"

The door opened and in
came the tall distin-
guished figure of the
Comptroller of the
Household. He bowed.

"Oh, good afternoon,
Sir Gregory," said the
Queen. "What can we do
for you?"

Is that the Royal "we", thought the Comptroller, or does she mean herself and the dog? "Forgive the intrusion, ma'am," he said, "but the Prince of Wales has just telephoned my office. He is passing through on his way from Highgrove to London and should be here very shortly."

"Thank you, Sir Gregory," said the Queen. "By the way, I don't think that you've met Titus."

"Titus, ma'am?"

"Yes, this little chap, my Prissy's last child. Titus, allow me to introduce Sir Gregory Collimore. Sir Gregory — Titus." She put the little chap down on the floor.

"How do you do, Titus?" said the Comptroller gravely, at which the young dog sat up on his bottom, paws held out before him, and Sir Gregory took hold of the right one and solemnly shook it.

"I've never known any of Your Majesty's corgis do that before, ma'am," he said.

"Nor have we," said the Queen.

Scarcely had the Comptroller left the room when the door opened once again, this time without a knock, and in came the Prince of Wales.

"Hullo, Charles," said the Queen.

"Hullo, Mummy," said Prince Charles, kissing his mother, and then "Who's this?" for Titus was still sitting up on his hunkers.

"His name is Titus," said the Queen.

"Never known any of your corgis do that before, Mummy. My terriers can't do that."

"Not surprised," said the Queen. "Tell me, why are you going to London?"

"Regimental dinner, Mummy. I am Colonel-in-Chief of the Welsh Guards, remember?"

The Queen smiled a rather patronizing smile. "Of course I remember, Charles," she said. "The most junior of the five regiments. As you no doubt remember, I happen to be Colonel-in-Chief of the Grenadiers, the most senior regiment in the Brigade of Guards."

The Prince of Wales laughed a somewhat uneasy laugh. "I shall have that job one day, Mummy," he said.

"When I'm dead and gone, you mean?"

"Well, er, yes."

"And you're King Charles the Third?"

"Well, er, yes."

Titus was still sitting up on his bottom and the Queen bent down and spoke softly in his ear. "He's going to have to wait an awfully long time," she whispered. "Specially if I live to be as old as my mum." And she giggled.

"What's funny, Mummy?" asked Prince Charles.

"Oh just a little joke between me and Titus."

"You talk as if he could understand what you're saying."

"He can, Charles, he can," said the Queen. "Now off you go to London, there's a good boy."

A little later, in the great drawing-room of Windsor Castle, the corgis sprang to attention, ears cocked, back ends wagging, as the Queen came in, carrying Titus.

"Sorry, Prissy," she said, putting the puppy down with his mother, "I couldn't bring your son back earlier because I had a visit from my son."

When she had gone out again, Prissy said to Titus, "Which son?"

"How d'you mean, Mum?"

"Well, Her Majesty . . ."

"Our servant, you mean?"

". . . yes, she has three sons. What did she call this one? Was it Edward?"

"No."

"Was it Andrew?"

"No."

"Then it must have been Charles."

"Yes, that was his name."

"He's the Prince of Wales, of course," said Prissy.

"So he's Welsh, like us?"

"No, he's English. Prince of Wales is his title. He'll be King of England when the Queen dies."

"He's going to have to wait an awfully long time," said Titus.

"Whatever d'you mean?"

"Well, that's what the servant told me."

"Oh Titus!" said Prissy. "What a lovely boy you are. How I do love you."

In an upstairs sitting-room Queen Elizabeth the Second was just settling down to read the Court Circular section of the *Daily Telegraph* when in came Prince Philip, Duke of Edinburgh, carrying a copy of *The Times*, open at Sport.

"Morning, Madge," he said.

"Good afternoon, Philip," his wife replied. "It's nearly one o'clock."

"Oh, is it?" said the Duke. "What's for lunch?"

"For you," said the Queen, "I've no idea. I'm having mine in here, on a tray. My favourites — Marmite sandwiches and cold rice pudding with strawberry jam."

"Ugh!" said the Duke. "Those corgis of yours get better grub than you do. You spoil 'em, Madge, especially that puppy you're always carrying around. Anyone would think he was Heir to the Throne. Which reminds me, Collimore tells me that Charles is here."

"He was. He's gone."

"Oh. All right, is he?"

"He didn't say."

"Hm," said Prince Philip. "Well, I must go and look for some lunch. Who knows, if I get down on all fours and wag my behind, maybe one of the footmen will bring me a nice plate of custard creams."

Chapter Six

Beyond knowing their names, Prince Philip knew nothing of the three footmen who came to answer any bell that he or the Queen might ring in Windsor Castle. When he spoke to one of them, to give an order, it was always in an abrupt manner, but then that was how he spoke to everyone.

The Queen did not know much more of them. She knew that Sidney, the one with fair curly hair, was from London, that John, black of hair and moustache, was a Scot, and that red-headed

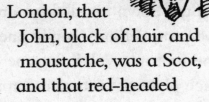

Patrick hailed from Ireland. When speaking to any of them, she was always civil, for she had been taught as a child that one should never never be rude to servants. But of their characters she knew nothing.

The three footmen were indeed very different, one from another. Patrick was a jolly fellow, always making jokes. He had an eye for the girls, and more than one of the maids that worked in the Castle had been winked at by the red-headed footman.

Though John, a quiet serious person, would never have dreamed of doing such a thing himself, he got on well with Patrick.

But neither the Scotsman nor the Irishman had any particular liking for fair, curly-headed Sidney, the third footman, who claimed to have been born in a rather smart part of London. He was indeed a smart-looking chap but Patrick and John somehow did not trust him too much.

Neither of them would have ever finished off any leftover coffee or biscuits, as Sidney always did, and each of them had, at one time or another, seen Sidney slip a couple of custard creams into his pocket before proceeding to the great drawing-room or to one of the Queen's sitting-rooms with a tray. Sidney, they agreed between themselves, was light-fingered. But they had no idea just how untrustworthy the Londoner was.

Nor had the Queen.

Until one fateful day when Sidney did something rather unwise and Titus won his spurs.

Time had flown, as it does, and Titus was now a year old, though the Queen still referred to him as "my puppy Titus".

"I'm not a puppy any more, am I, Mum?" he said to his mother.

"No, dear," replied Prissy. "You are a grown-up corgi and a very handsome one too. No wonder the servant spoils you like she does. Why, you'll be sleeping on her bed next, I shouldn't wonder."

By now Titus knew his way around the Castle pretty well, and though he'd never actually been in the Queen's bedroom, he knew where it was. That afternoon he trotted along, through passages and

corridors and up flights of stairs, until he came to its door which, rather to his surprise, was ajar. He peeped into the room and there, at the Queen's dressing-table, was the fair-haired footman.

As Titus watched, Sidney picked up a silver box (a jewel-case it was, could Titus have known) and opened its lid and peered inside. Something told Titus that this was wrong. The man shouldn't be there in the Royal bedroom, he felt sure, and he gave a little growl.

Sidney swung round, hastily closing the jewel-case. Then, seeing Titus standing alone in the doorway, he heaved a sigh of relief.

"Blimey, you gave me a fright, you little fattie!" he said. "I've got a good mind to kick your fat backside." And he made a move towards Titus, who ran off, barking.

A couple of hours later, Sidney sat in the saloon bar of a backstreet Windsor pub, in company with a rather flashily-dressed middle-aged man. They sat in a far corner, talking quietly over their pints.

"It'll be as easy as pie, Percy," said Sidney. "She hadn't even locked it."

"You're sure it's hers, Sid?" asked the man, Percy.

"Course it's hers. It's in her bedroom. And it's crammed full of jewels. Rings, brooches,

earrings, neck‐
laces, worth a
fortune they must
be. Soon as I saw 'em, I thought of you,
Perce. Old Perce the fence, I said to myself,
he'll place 'em for me. She'll never even
notice they're gone. It's a piece of cake."

"Slow down, slow down, Sid," said Percy.
"Nice and easy does it, you don't want to
go taking too much at a time. Just pick a
few things for a start, mind."

"And we'll split what they fetch, 50–50,
Perce?"

"60 to me, Sid, 40 to you. I've got to place
them."

"But I've got to nick them!"

"Piece of cake, you said."

"Well, yes, she's gone up to Buckingham
Palace with old Phil, but it's risky all the same."

"You just go and get them, Sid," said the
fence. "Just a few small things you can put in
your pockets. I'll meet you back here later."

*

And so it was that later that evening the fair-haired footman Sidney made his cautious way up to the bedroom of Her Majesty Queen Elizabeth the Second. Because the Queen was not in residence, many of the servants, including John and Patrick, were taking time off, and even Sir Gregory Collimore had put his feet up. But there was someone who was still on duty.

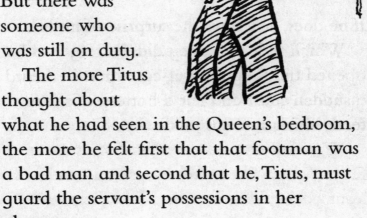

The more Titus thought about what he had seen in the Queen's bedroom, the more he felt first that that footman was a bad man and second that he, Titus, must guard the servant's possessions in her absence.

He did not consult his mother about this (I'm not a puppy any more, he thought) but in turn made his cautious way up to Her Majesty's bedroom and crept under Her Majesty's great four-poster bed and curled up comfortably on Her Majesty's thick carpet.

If the man doesn't come back, he thought, I'll have a jolly good sleep.

If he does, he'll have the surprise of his life.

Which indeed Sidney did. Hardly had he opened the Royal jewel-case than he heard a sudden snarl and felt a battery of sharp teeth biting into his ankle.

Chapter Seven

"GERRIMOFF! GERRIMOFF!!"

It was a passing maid who first heard the frantic yells coming from the Queen's bedroom, and she ran to tell other members of staff, and they alerted the officer commanding the Castle guard, and he telephoned the Comptroller of Her Majesty's Household. Sir Gregory arrived at the doorway of the Royal bedroom to see before him an extraordinary sight.

Inside there stood an officer of the Grenadier Guards and half a dozen guardsmen, weapons at the ready. Scattered all over the carpet, Sir Gregory could see, were rings and brooches and earrings and necklaces and a silver jewel-case, open and empty. Amongst all these valuables Sidney the footman hopped and howled, one of his ankles held, in a bulldog grip, by a furiously growling corgi.

"Gerrimoff!" he still cried feebly, and at a signal from the officer, one of the guardsmen laid down his rifle and knelt and managed to prise open the dog's jaws and thus release the prisoner. And a prisoner of course Sidney was destined to be, for his guilt was plain to the onlookers (and indeed his pockets were full of rings) and, in due course, to the judge.

The footman had been caught in the act of stealing the Queen's jewels, and caught, what's more, by the cunning and courage of one of Her Majesty's corgis.

After the soldiers had taken the man away to be placed in police custody, Sir Gregory Collimore went to his office to report the matter by telephone to the Queen at Buckingham Palace.

"Nabbed him, did he, Sir Gregory?" she said. "Got him by the ankle, eh?"

"Yes, ma'am. The man's leg was quite severely lacerated, I understand."

"Serve him right," said the Queen. "Which of my corgis did the deed?"

"I am told it was the one to whom Your Majesty formally introduced me, some months ago. His name, as I recall, ma'am, is Titus."

"My Titus!" cried the Queen. "I'll come straight back! I must reward him!"

Reward him? Sir Gregory thought to himself as he put down the phone. What's she going to do – give him a medal? It'll have to be the D.C.M. (Distinguished Corgi Medal), and he left his office, smiling at his own joke.

In the Palace, the Queen put down her receiver and turned to the Duke of Edinburgh. "Did you hear that, Philip?" she said.

"How could I hear it, Madge?" Prince Philip replied. "You answered the phone, not me. But I gathered that one of your wretched corgis had bitten someone."

"It was Titus. He nabbed one of the foot-men. Bit him."

"In the foot?"

"No, in the ankle. In my bedroom."

"Why? Hadn't the man given him enough custard creams?"

"Don't be silly, Philip. He was robbing my jewel-case."

"Who, the corgi?"

"No, the footman, of course."

"Which one?"

"Sidney."

"Is that the fair-haired one, Madge?"

"Yes."

"Never liked the cut of his jib," said Prince Philip. "Eyes too close together. And his ears – too small. Never trust a chap with small ears. Always knew he was a phoney."

"Anyway," said the Queen, "we are going straight back to Windsor."

"We?"

"I am going straight back."

"Oh I see. It was the Royal 'we'."

"Philip," said the Queen coldly. "We are not amused."

As soon as she arrived back at Windsor Castle, the Queen went into the great drawing-room, where all her corgis were, as usual, gathered. All, as usual, got off armchairs and sofas and assembled around the Royal ankles, ears flattened, bottoms waggling, but on this day the Queen had eyes for one only.

"Titus!" she said. "You are a hero!" And she tugged at a long bell-pull that hung beside the fireplace.

The black-moustached footman knocked and entered.

"Custard creams, please, John," said the Queen. "Nine of them. Plus three chocolate digestives. And a pot of tea for me."

Chapter Eight

As Titus grew up, he found that not everyone was easy to get on with. Always he
tried hard to behave with the same polite-
ness and good manners as his servant the
Queen did. But the day came when he
once more used his teeth in anger.

One particular corgi called Chum never
lived up to his name because he wasn't
very friendly to anyone, especially Titus.

When Titus had first been allowed into the great drawing-room, much earlier than puppies usually were, Chum had taken an instant dislike to him.

At first it was just a matter of seniority. Chum was at that time two years old, and he thought that Prissy's son was too bumptious by half. He growled and showed his teeth whenever Titus came near.

But then, once it became obvious to all the corgis that Titus was well on the way to becoming the Queen's favourite, it was, for Chum, a matter of pure jealousy. Why should this whippersnapper be so spoiled?

For Chum, worse was to come, for after Titus's encounter with the burgling footman, the Queen broke all her previous rules.

She allowed Titus to sleep on the end of her bed at nights. Prissy, of course, was very proud when this happened, and most of the others didn't much mind, but there were some who feared that this privilege would give Titus a swelled head, and Chum was especially narked.

One day, by chance, he met Titus in a corridor, and his feelings boiled over. "Hey you!" he growled at Titus, who was about to pass peacefully by. "I want a word with you, you cocky little pup!"

"Excuse me," said Titus politely. "I am no longer a puppy. I am an adult corgi."

"Adult, are you?" snarled Chum. "Old enough to defend yourself then?"

"Defend myself?" said Titus. "Against whom?"

"Against me," Chum replied. "I'm fed up to the back teeth" (and he showed them) "with you and your airs and graces. Think yourself special, don't you? Think you're a cut above the rest of us, eh?"

"No, I don't."

"Sleeping on the Queen's bed, eh?" went on Chum. "How d'you get up on it, then?"

"The servant lifts me up."

"Servant? What servant?"

"The Queen. Mum says she is our servant."

"Oh she says that, does she?" growled Chum. He took a pace forward, so that their noses were almost touching. "Well all I can say is – your mother's a silly old fool."

This was too much for Titus. Up to that point he'd been hoping to avoid a fight with the older dog, and even thinking that it might perhaps be wise to run for it, back to the safety of the great drawing-room. But to hear his beloved mother called "a silly old fool"!

"How dare you say that!" he cried, and he sank his teeth into one of Chum's ears.

The noise of the fight rang down the long corridors, to be clearly heard by all the other corgis, by the two footmen, by the Comptroller of Her Majesty's Household, by Prince Philip, Duke of Edinburgh – and finally by Queen Elizabeth herself. All in turn hastened to the scene.

First came Prissy, loudly barking "Mummy's coming, darling!" and followed by the rest of the pack.

Then John of the black moustache and Patrick of the red hair came running, followed, as quickly as he could manage, by a hurrying Sir Gregory Collimore.

Then "What the devil's going on?" shouted a loud voice as Prince Philip arrived. By now all the corgis had joined in the scuffle, and both the footmen had been nipped while trying to break it up, and Sir Gregory, a little dizzy from his unaccustomed haste, had unfortunately tripped up Prince Philip, so that both fell to the floor.

Then suddenly a high-pitched voice cried loudly "QUIET!" and lo, there was quiet, for not one of the corgis would have dreamt of disobeying such a Royal Command. The Queen stood, hands on hips, surveying the scene.

Several of her dogs were licking at nipped paws or torn ears, her footmen were trying to bandage with handkerchiefs their sore fingers, and on the floor of the corridor sprawled the prostrate figures of her breathless Comptroller and her furious Consort.

But she had eyes for only one. "Titus!" she called. "Are you all right?"

Chapter Nine

The damage to Titus, the Queen found,
was very little. Prissy and the other corgis
had mostly pitched in to poor Chum, who
was looking rather the worse for wear. As
well as having had an ear quite badly
bitten by Titus (from then on it always
drooped a bit), he had had a
number of nips to nose and
paws, and the Queen spent
some time attending to him
that evening. She also com-
manded the two footmen to
see a doctor, and she made
sure that her elderly Comptroller
was none the worse for his fall.

Not till all this was done did she go to enquire after her husband. "You didn't hurt yourself, did you, Philip?" she asked when they met in her sitting-room.

"Luckily, no."

"How did you come to fall?"

"Old Collimore tripped me up," replied the Duke of Edinburgh. "Wasn't his fault, it was all due to those blasted corgis of yours, Madge. I expect that one you call Titus started it. I just wish you'd get rid of the whole pack of them."

"Get rid of them?" said the Queen.

"Yes, give 'em away to someone. Why don't you give 'em to Charles? They're Welsh, he's the Prince of Wales, send 'em all down to Highgrove. Or give 'em to Anne. Or Andrew. Or Edward. Or whatshername, the Duchess of Thingamajig, you know?"

The Queen drew herself up to her full modest height. "Generally speaking, Philip," she said in an icy voice, "you do not forget yourself to this extent. May I remind you that I am Queen of England and will not be spoken to in this way. How dare you suggest that I should part with my beloved corgis!"

"Only joking, Madge," said her husband.

"A joke," said the Queen, "in the poorest of taste." And she swept out of the room.

Left to himself, Prince Philip stood, wryly regarding his reflection in a looking-glass on the wall. "Well, well," he said. "The old girl still packs a pretty good broadside. It's a wonder she didn't tell me to 'Sit!' or 'Stay!'" He rang a bell.

Shortly, there was a knock on the door. "Come in!" shouted the Duke, and in came the red-haired footman, two of his fingers bandaged. The duke looked at him thoughtfully.

"Are you married?" he asked.

"Married, Your Royal Highness?" said Patrick. "No, sir, I am not."

"Well take my advice and don't bother. Or if you do, make sure that you're master in your own house. Now, get me a drink and run me a nice hot bath. I've had enough of today."

When the Queen returned later, she found the red-haired footman on his knees, making up the fire. He sprang to his feet.

"Where is Prince Philip, Patrick?" the Queen asked.

The Duke of Edinburgh's private bathroom chanced to be immediately above that particular sitting-room in Windsor Castle, and the footman instinctively gave an upward look at the ceiling as he answered, "His Royal Highness is taking a bath, Your Majesty."

72

"Thank you, Patrick," said the Queen. "You may leave the fire now, I'll see to it. How are your fingers, by the way?"

"Sure they're fine, ma'am, thank you, ma'am."

"And John's had his seen to?"

"Yes, ma'am. The doctor bandaged us both up. A nasty nip he said it was," the footman told her, and he bowed and left the room, backwards.

The Queen sat down and patted her lap and Titus jumped up on to it. "What a dreadful business! Whoever nipped the footmen's fingers, I'm sure it wasn't you, dear boy. It was probably poor old Chum. I wonder what that rumpus was all about? Pity you can't tell me."

Somehow Titus had a pretty good idea what the servant was saying. I'm sure you'd understand why I went for Chum, he thought. You'd do the same if someone had called your mother a silly old fool.

The Queen and her dog sat comfortably together before the fire, and before long the Royal eyes began to close. What with one thing and another, it had been a rather exhausting day for Her Majesty, and she dozed off. Titus, too, felt tired after the fight and, as he happily settled on the Royal lap, he sleepily thought, now I'm a lapdog. He was about to take a snooze when suddenly he heard a noise.

It was only a little noise, a sort of *plop*, the sound a drip of water makes. He opened his eyes and saw that there was indeed a drip of water falling on to the carpet of the sitting-room. He looked up and saw another drop fall, and another, and another, until there was a steady stream of water falling from a rapidly growing patch of damp on the ceiling, that ceiling that was directly below Prince Philip's private bathroom.

Chapter Ten

Something's up! thought Titus, or rather something's down! He began to bark. The Royal eyes opened smartly, to see what could only now be called a waterfall. Leaping from her chair, the Queen ran for the door with Titus at her heels.

Prince Philip's bath was not the usual sort. It had belonged to his wife's great-great-grand-mother, Queen Victoria. She had been very short, so her bath was very short too, which suited the Duke of Edinburgh well, for even

though he was tall, he liked to sit up in the
tub. Which was just as well, for if, on that
particular evening, he had been lying down
in it as most people do, then the Queen
would very probably have soon been
referred to – as her great-great-grand-
mother had been – as The Widow
of Windsor.

As it was, the Duke sat
up in his bath water, a large
glass of whisky in the soap
dish by his side, and reflected
upon the events of the day. Madge and her
wretched corgis, he thought. Lazy fat
spoiled little brutes. All the same, there was
one of them with a bit of character, that
one that had caught the burgling footman.
What was the dog's name?
Ah yes, Titus, that was it.

After a while the bath
water grew a little cool, and
the Duke turned on the taps
again. But then, lulled by the

warm water and the whisky, he began to feel rather sleepy. His chin dropped upon his chest, and the sound of his snores mingled with the splashing of water from the two still running bath taps.

Gradually the level in Queen Victoria's bath rose, till it reached the overflow. Then, because the overflow couldn't cope with the volume of water, it rose higher, to the rim of the bath, over the rim of the bath, and began to spill on to the floor. Through it all Prince Philip slept peacefully, till he was suddenly woken by a volley of barking coming from the room directly below. Not for nothing had the Prince served his time in the Royal Navy.

Open the seacock! he thought, and he yanked the plug out, and then with a loud shout of "Abandon ship!" he leapt out of the bath.

Hastily wrapping himself in a large towel, he paddled across the sodden floor. As he reached the bathroom door, it was flung open, and there stood the figure of the Queen, at her heels a single corgi.

"Sorry, Madge," the Duke said damply. "I dropped off to sleep in the tub. Some dog barking woke me up."

"This dog woke you up," replied the Queen. "This dog, my Titus. If it hadn't been for his watchfulness, the ceiling would probably have come down on top of us. Frankly, Philip, I have to say that we are not amused."

Then she looked again at the tall figure of her Consort, standing barefooted on the squelchy floor, clutching his damp bath towel around him, and dripping.

She began to hoot with laughter.

Chapter Eleven

Bewildered, Titus made his own way back
to the great drawing-room. Humans, he
thought as he went, I don't understand
them. I mean, look at our servant just now
– one minute she was angry, the next she
was laughing her head off. Perhaps it's
because they're Royals, maybe they're
different from other people. They must be if
you think about it because everybody else
treats them quite differently. I mean, look at

the footmen, they go out of the room backwards, and the maids, they curtsey, and Sir Gregory, he bows. Royal people must be very special.

I wonder if Royal dogs are too? After all, we corgis are the Queen's dogs, so maybe we're all princes and princesses. Prince Titus, how does that sound? Actually, I think I'd rather be a king amongst dogs. King Titus the First. Yes, that's more like it.

"Wherever have you been?" Prissy asked her son when he came into the room. "You're all wet, your paws are soaking."

All the other corgis gathered round Titus while he explained what had been going on.

"The bath water came right through the ceiling, you say?" Prissy asked.

"Yes, right down into the Queen's sitting-room."

"But why," asked one of the other dogs, "hadn't Prince Philip turned the taps off?"

"He went to sleep in the bath," Titus replied.

"And she was angry with him?" asked someone else.

"Yes, very."

"But then she started laughing, you say?" said another.

'Yes," said Titus. "I don't understand people. They don't seem to act normally, like dogs do."

"Well, dogs get angry sometimes, don't they?" said Prissy. "You did, with Chum."

"That wasn't anything to laugh at," growled Chum, and he continued, unsuccessfully, to try to lick his injured ear.

"Anyway," said Prissy, "if I've got the story right, it was your barking that woke both of them up."

"Yes," said Titus.

"You seem to be making quite a name for yourself, my son," Prissy said. "First catching a burglar, and now giving the alarm and saving the situation. What next,

81

I wonder? If you keep on like this, you won't only be sleeping on the Queen's bed, you'll be eating off her plate, I shouldn't be surprised."

At that moment the Queen came into the room. All the dogs crowded round her, and she gave each a pat and a special stroking to Chum ("How's your poor ear feeling, old boy?") and to Prissy ("How does it feel to be the mother of a hero, eh?").

Then she rang the bell and when the black-moustached footman came in, she said, "Take all the dogs out on to the lawn, please, John." When that had been done, the Queen ordered custard creams all round (with an extra chocolate digestive for the hero) and when those had been eaten, she said "Right, everybody, bedtime!" and nine corgis settled themselves comfortably in armchairs and on sofas, while the tenth and youngest followed Her Majesty as she made her way to the State Bedroom.

Once she herself was comfortably settled, the Queen turned out her bedside light. She yawned. Then she wiggled her toes against the warm shape that lay on the end of her bed. "G'night, Titus," she said sleepily. "I may be a Queen among my people but you're a king among my dogs."

Chapter Twelve

For most of his long life Sir Gregory Collimore had been in the service of the Royal Family, and for many years now he had been Comptroller of the Queen's household at Windsor Castle. But for most of his long life, Sir Gregory had had a very bad habit. He smoked cigarettes, lots of them, every day. And one day before Titus was so very much older, Sir Gregory's bad habit almost caused a disaster.

It happened like this.

The Comptroller came out of his office, closing the door behind him, and made his rather slow way along the corridors towards his private quarters. In an ashtray on his office desk lay the end of his latest cigarette. Maybe he had forgotten to stub it out, maybe he hadn't stubbed it out properly, but it was still alight.

Then a little puff of wind came in through the open window, and the cigarette end rolled off the ashtray and onto some papers that lay on the desk. By a lucky chance Titus was on his way from the Queen's sitting-room to the great drawing-room, to pay a visit to his mother and all the other corgis, when he smelled smoke. A dog's sense of smell is many many times sharper than a human's, and it was immediately plain to Titus that something was burning.

That was nothing unusual, for there were dozens of fires of coal or logs all over Windsor Castle. But this smell, Titus's nose told him, was not of coal or logs. It was of burning paper. Just as he had been in the matter of the burgling footman and the overflowing bath, Titus was immediately on the alert. Something, he knew, was wrong. Someone must be told about it. At that precise moment Prince Philip came in sight, marching along the corridor, and Titus turned and ran towards him. Now though he cordially disliked almost all his wife's dogs, there was something about this particular one that had rather taken the Duke's fancy, and he said (in quite a pleasant voice), "Hullo there, Titus. What's the hurry?"

By now the smell of burning paper was very strong in the dog's little nose though it had not yet reached the man's much bigger one, and in his anxiety Titus began to tug at the Royal trouser turn-ups.

"Belay that!" growled the Duke of Edinburgh. "What the devil d'you think you're playing at?" But Titus continued to tug and to whine and then to run a little way towards the burning smell and then back, again and again, till at last the Duke got the message and followed. Now he too smelled the smoke and broke into a run. Titus ran directly to the door of Sir Gregory Collimore's office and scratched at it, and the Duke flung it open, to see a great many papers burning merrily away on the Comptroller's desk, itself now alight. Now was the moment when Prince Philip's naval training came into play.

"England expects every man will do his duty!" he shouted, and his duty indeed he did, regardless of his own safety. There was no fire-party to be summoned nor fire-hoses to be brought to bear, as there would have been on board ship. But the Duke saw immediately that, in the absence of water, the growing fire must quickly be smothered. But with what? There was no handy rug – the floor of the Comptroller's office was close-carpeted – but on the wall behind, there hung above the burning desk a large picture, a portrait of Sir Gregory Collimore in full ceremonial dress.

Quickly the Duke of Edinburgh yanked the portrait from its hangings and somehow found the strength (for it was very heavy) to slam the painted Sir Gregory down upon the fire, face first, and thus to extinguish the flames.

"Phew!" he said, mopping his Royal brow. "That could have been very nasty, Titus. In fact, if it hadn't been for you, it *would* have been very nasty. Come on, old chap, we'll go and tell Madge. This will be worth a good few custard creams to you. Might even get one myself if I'm lucky."

When the Queen was told, her first thought was for her favourite. "You're not hurt, Titus, are you?" she said. "You haven't burned your paws?"

"I put the fire out, you know, Madge," said the Duke in a rather hurt voice. He held out his hands, black from his firefighting efforts. "And my paws are dirty."

"Yes, yes, Philip, so you said. But it was my clever little Titus that gave the alarm again." She rang for a footman.

When the custard creams came, she began to feed them to Titus, disregarding the ten pairs of eyes (nine corgis and a Duke) that were watching hungrily.

"He's a king among dogs, don't you think, Philip?" she said.

"Well, I'm a Prince among men."

"Oh all right," said the Queen. "You can have one if you like."

Chapter Thirteen

Later that day Queen Elizabeth the Second and her husband Prince Philip, Duke of Edinburgh, sat watching television together, as many elderly couples do. This couple, however, seldom did, their tastes in viewing being very different, but now something seemed to have made them more companionable. They sat side by side upon a sofa, between them the plump brown body of Titus, and the Queen suddenly noticed that her husband was absently fondling the dog's big ears.

"Never seen you do that before, Philip," she said.

"Do what?"

"Make a fuss of any of my corgis."

"Hm," said the Duke. "Well as you know, Madge, they aren't my favourite animals. But I've taken rather a shine to this chap. Remarkable little beast, really."

The Queen put a hand to her face to hide a smile. They were watching a documentary about vandalism in inner-city areas and there was a shot of a public building, its wall liberally daubed with graffiti in large white letters. Some of the words were rather rude, at which the Queen looked disapproving and the Duke guffawed.

Many of the messages had something in common.

Man Utd rules OK.

T. Blair rules OK.

Jeremy Paxman rules OK.

Posh and Becks rule OK.

and so on and so forth.

"What's all that?" asked the Queen testily. "I'm the only person who rules. OK?"

"I know, Madge, I know," said Prince Philip, and he put a hand to his face to hide a grin.

"How do they write these stupid messages?" asked the Queen.

"With spraycans of paint, I believe," her husband replied. "Kind of an aerosol gadget, you just press a button and it squirts out."

"Ridiculous!" said the Queen. "Vandalism like that is so mindless. Imagine doing such a thing."

"I can't imagine you doing it, Madge," the Duke said.

"As if I would!" snorted the Queen.

That night, as she settled herself for sleep, she addressed the warm shape lying against her feet at the bottom of her bed. "As if I would, Titus," she said, and after a moment a small smile flickered across the Royal features.

Next morning she sent for one of her Ladies-in-Waiting. "Would you be good enough," she said to her, "to do a little shopping for me?"

"Of course, ma'am," replied the Lady-in-Waiting. "What was it that you wanted?"

"I think they're called spraycans," the Queen said. "They squirt paint. I want to decorate something."

The Lady-in-Waiting looked puzzled. "Er, what colour would you like, ma'am?" she asked.

"Golden, please."

That night the soldiers on guard at Windsor Castle patrolled as usual around the various buildings, pausing beneath the windows of the Queen's sitting-room, opposite which, on the other side of a courtyard, was a large blank wall. Not until they had marched out of sight did a shadowy figure emerge, carrying an object, and approach the wall.

Next morning Prince Philip was woken early by his wife, on whom Titus was, as usual, in attendance.

"Come and have a look, Philip," said the Queen. "We want to show you something."

Grumbling, the Duke followed her into her sitting-room. "Show me what?" he growled.

"Have a look outside," said the Queen, and he went to the window and looked out, and there on the wall opposite was written in huge golden capital letters

"Good grief!" said the Duke. "Who did that?"

"I did."

"You did, Madge?"

"Yes," said the Queen, fondly stroking her favourite corgi. "I told you, Phil, he's a king among dogs, aren't you, Titus?"

Prince Philip shook his head in wonderment. "Madge, old girl," he said. "How could you do such a thing?"

"With this, of course," replied the Queen, producing the spraycan. "It was such fun, Phil. In fact, with all due respect to Great-great-grandmama, we are quite definitely amused." And then they both burst out laughing.